Ava and the Mermaid Club

A MERMAID GIRLS CHAPTER BOOK

A.M. Luzzader

ILLUSTRATED BY
CHADD VANZANTEN

Published by Knowledge Forest Press
P.O. Box 6331
Logan, UT 84341

Ebook ISBN-13: 978-1-949078-71-8
Paperback ISBN-13: 978-1-949078-80-0

Cover design by Beautiful Book Covers (beetifulbookcovers.com)

Editing by Chadd VanZanten

Interior illustrations by Chadd VanZanten

For Addi, happy reading!

Contents

Chapter One

You PROBABLY KNOW that there is a magical world just beneath the ocean's surface. It's magical because of all the wondrous places, like coral reefs. It's magical because of the many kinds of sea life, like whales, octopuses, and sea cucumbers. (Yes, sea cucumbers are real.)

But the oceans are magical for another reason.

The undersea world is also magical because it's where merfolk live. These mer people use their mermagical powers to protect the oceans. They make sure that the undersea plant and animal life is safe and taken care of, including sea cucumbers.

The world of merfolk is similar to the world of humans on land. We have friends and families on land. Merfolk have families and friends in their underwater world. We have houses and schools on land. The merfolk have houses and schools, too, though they are usually in underwater caves.

When mermaids and merboys turn twelve or thirteen years of age, they learn special mermagical spells that they use to help take care of the ocean. Young merkids aren't able to cast lots of mermagical spells, but all merfolk are naturally magical. They all know a little magic.

In the human world, all people are different and unique. It's the same with merfolk. Some mers have brown or black hair. Others might have pink or purple hair.

Merfolk do not have feet or legs, of course. They are very different from humans in this way. Merfolk have tails and fins, which allow them to swim. Their tails have sparkly scales that shimmer like glitter. Merfolk tails can be blue or green. They can be black or pink. They can even be blue, green, black, and pink on the same tail. Merfolk tails can be any color of the rainbow.

Merfolk also come in all different sizes, just like us. Some are short. Some are skinny. Some are curvy.

This story is about a mermaid who was quite tall.

Her name was Ava Gillie. Her tail was bluish-silver with purple highlights. Ava also had short brown hair with bangs and brown eyes.

Ava wasn't old enough yet to know how to do any magical spells, but she still tried to make the ocean a better place where she could. If she ever saw any litter or garbage, she always cleaned it up. Or if she saw a younger mermaid or merboy who was lost and needed help, she'd stop what she was doing to help them find their way. Ava made friends easily, and she loved spending time with other mers.

One day, Ava stood in front of her bedroom mirror, trying on different swim tops. She put on a gray one, then took it off and threw it across the room.

"How about the green one?" Ava said to herself. She slipped into the green swim top, but then she took it off and threw it on her bed.

Ava's pet catfish, Tom, swam around the bedroom, dodging the clothes as they flew through the room.

Ava put on a swim top with red and blue stripes. "How does this one look, Tom?" she asked.

Tom twitched his whiskers and flicked his tail. Ava wasn't sure if that meant he liked it or not.

Ava looked at herself in the mirror again and tilted her head. Then she sighed. "There's just something about it I don't quite like."

Tom swam slowly around the room, sniffing at the growing pile of Ava's clothes.

Ava frowned. She had tried on almost every swim top in her closet. A lot of her clothes were too small. Ava had grown a lot lately.

"You're getting so tall!" Ava's mother and father said proudly.

But even some of the clothes that fit Ava perfectly didn't seem right. Ava didn't like them anymore.

"It's all because I'm so tall," Ava said quietly. "I'm too tall."

It might be better to say Ava was "long." If a fisherman caught a big fish, he would probably say the fish were "long" instead of "tall." But it was true that Ava was tall for her age. And she was still growing taller. She was taller than all of the mermaids in her school class. She was taller than most of the merboys.

Humans and merfolk are sometimes unhappy about the way they look. This is perfectly normal. Some humans think their noses are too big. Some merfolk think their tails are too small. Some humans think they are too round. Some merfolk think they are too skinny.

Ava didn't know or understand that everyone grows at their own speed. This is true for humans and merfolk. Ava didn't seem to know that some mermaids grew faster than others. She also didn't seem to know that everyone is unique. Everyone is different. Being tall was one of the things that made Ava special.

But Ava didn't think about that. She didn't think

she was special or unique. She thought she was just too tall.

I wish I wasn't so tall, Ava thought. *I wish I was normal looking, like everyone else.*

If Ava thought more about this, she would have understood that there's really no such thing as "normal looking." Everyone looks different. Even people who look alike are different in small ways. And besides, if everyone looked the same, the world would not be very interesting or fun.

But Ava didn't think of any of that. Instead, she finally picked a swim top to wear. She didn't like it very much, so she put on a heavy jacket, too. She hoped this might make her look less tall. She hoped no one would notice how tall she was.

Ava gave herself one last look in the mirror. She still didn't like the outfit she wore.

"This will just have to do," she told Tom. "I don't want to miss the Mermaid Club meeting. I'll just have to try to not look so tall."

Chapter Two

Ava did not love the clothes in her closet, but she loved Mermaid Club.

The club was created by Ava's friend Chloe. Mermaid Club was a group that anyone could join. The members of the club did fun activities and service projects together.

Ava loved Mermaid Club because it brought everyone together. It was a great way for merkids to meet and be friends. The club also did fun things. Together they did things that Ava had never done before. They visited the older merfolk at the Sunny Oceans Senior Living Center. They'd also gone to a mermagical show at the theater.

At first, Mermaid Club had only three members.

It was Chloe, Ava, and their friend Emma. Since then, more members had joined Mermaid Club. Chloe was the president of the club. Ava was the vice president. Ava's job was to help with club meetings and plan activities for the club.

"Everyone is welcome!" Chloe had said. She and Ava had been talking to other merkids and asking them to join.

Today the Mermaid Club was planning their next activity. The meeting was held at a shady spot near the kelp forest, where sea otters and schools of silvery fish swam around. Colorful sea urchins crawled around below. It was a beautiful and peaceful place. The kelp forest reminded Ava of a library because it was quiet and peaceful, except it wasn't in a building and there were no books.

When Ava arrived at the meeting, she was still feeling awkward about her height. Ava was the first mer to arrive. She quickly swam in and sat on a rock.

Maybe if I sit down, Ava thought, *no one will notice how tall I'm growing.* Ava worried that people would think unkind thoughts about her if they saw how tall she had grown.

A few minutes later, Chloe arrived.

"Ava! I'm glad you're here!" said Chloe cheerfully. "I printed up an agenda for our meeting."

She gave Ava a stack of papers.

"This is a list of everything we'll discuss today," said Chloe. "Would you mind giving them to everyone?"

Ordinarily Ava would have been happy to help. She was impressed that Chloe had prepared the agendas for the meeting, but other merkids were starting to arrive for the meeting.

"Um, sure," said Ava, but she really didn't want to.

Ava gave the agendas to everyone who came to the meeting. She tried to hunch over, to make herself shorter, like Chloe. Chloe was quite short for her age. Ava hunched over more. She was worried that if she and Chloe were both swimming around at the same time, everyone would notice how tall she was.

I look like a giant when I swim next to Chloe, thought Ava.

But Mermaid Club was Ava's favorite thing. She wanted to help. Besides, Ava was the vice president, and she liked being around the other members of the club. So, Ava swam around the meeting area, giving the agendas to everyone. But still she hunched over, keeping her tail bent. This made it hard to swim.

Ava's friend Emma arrived at the meeting. Emma had wavy brown hair and pretty brown eyes. Her tail was orange, and her scales glittered with yellow and pink. She took a seat on a rock in the meeting area.

"Hi, Ava!" said Emma.

"Hi, Emma!" said Ava.

Ava gave Emma a meeting agenda. Emma was the

club secretary. It was her job to write down everything that happened at Mermaid Club meetings and activities.

Emma looked at Ava with a curious expression. Then she said, "Ava, is something wrong?"

Oh, no! thought Ava. *She knows I'm trying to hide how tall I am!"*

"Wrong?" said Ava. "No, nothing's wrong. What do you mean?"

Emma frowned and said, "Well, you're wearing a heavy jacket when it is very warm. You also seem to be scrunching yourself down."

"Who, me?" asked Ava. "No, nothing's wrong. I just felt a cool current earlier and got cold."

"What about the scrunching?" asked Emma.

"Scrunching?" replied Ava. "Who's scrunching? Not me!"

But of course she was crouching and scrunching and stooping, and this made it difficult for her to swim properly.

Just then, a school of huge grouper fish swam over their heads.

Each one was nearly as big as a mer-kid. They weren't dangerous. They were just very large and slow.

They swam over the Mermaid Club meeting. Ava tried to scrunch down even more, but she was simply too tall, and several of the grouper fish bumped into Ava's head. She let go of the agenda papers, and they flew through the water in every direction. This scared the grouper fish, and they swam through the Mermaid Club meeting.

Emma sprang up from her seat to help. The papers swirled around the kelp forest. Giant grouper fish were swimming everywhere. All of this commotion frightened some squids who were resting nearby in the kelp. They burst out of their resting place and also swam through the meeting. They had large, round eyes, which made them seem even more afraid.

Squids and octopuses have an interesting ability. When they are frightened, they squirt clouds of dark ink into the water. The ink clouds confuse their enemies and it helps them get away.

That is what the squids did when the grouper fish frightened them. They squirted their ink. Now the water around the meeting area was filled with floating papers, giant grouper fish, and swirling clouds of squid ink! Some of the club members tried to help. However, some of the new members thought it was part of the meeting, so they swam around, chasing each other. This frightened even more squids from the kelp, and now the water became almost black with squid ink! There was laughing and shouting and confusion everywhere.

"Oh, no!" cried Chloe. "This meeting is falling apart!"

It's all my fault, thought Ava. *It's because I'm so tall, and I was trying to hide it!*

Working together, the Mermaid Club members collected all the papers and chased away the groupers. The squids were gone, and the ink clouds drifted away.

"Ava, are you okay?" Emma asked.

Ava's cheeks burned. *Not only am I tall,* she thought, *I'm also a klutz!*

"Yeah," said Chloe. "Are you all right?"

"I'm okay," said Ava. All she wanted to do was to get back to her seat.

"Why were you swimming like that?" Emma asked.

Ava felt very embarrassed. She frowned. "You mean why am I so tall and clumsy?"

Emma made a face. "No, not because you're tall, just because you were swimming strangely."

It's because I'm so tall! thought Ava.

Several merkids were still chasing around the area and laughing.

Chloe swam to the front of the club and shouted, "Okay, everyone! Settle down. That was not official club business! Please take your seats so that we can start the meeting!"

After a while, everyone was sitting down and paying attention.

"Thank you," said Chloe. "Today we're going to discuss our upcoming events. We will also make assignments for what needs to be done."

Ava settled into her seat and smiled. At last, she could enjoy the Mermaid Club meeting. She was the vice president, but she didn't know what the next activity was.

"Our next activity," Chloe said, "will be a square dance at Fishy Fun Dance Hall. Jillian Seagull's dad has volunteered to show us how to do the square dances!"

In square dancing, four dance partners stand in a square. The square dance moves are called out by an instructor. The instructor might tell them to circle to the left, or they might twirl to the right. The dancers do whatever the instructor calls out. That's the way humans do square dancing. However, merfolk take square dancing to a whole new level. This is because merfolk can swim through the water. They can dance upwards and downwards. They can do back flips and front flips. They use bubbles in their dancing. Merfolk dancers can even dance upside down!

"Mr. Seagull will also call out the dancing instructions!" said Chloe.

Ava had gone to a mer dance before with her parents when she was a lot younger. She liked it a lot. Ava remembered having a lot of fun. She thought, *Cool! A square dance! This will be super fun!* Many of the other members of Mermaid Club were also excited to hear about the square dance. They clapped and chattered excitedly.

But then Ava realized something.

At a dance, Ava thought, *everyone must have a partner. I will probably be taller than my partner. I'll be embarrassed! Everyone will stare at me!*

This made Ava feel sad and nervous. Ava always loved being around lots of merkids and merfolk. She loved big, noisy events like dances and parties. But now she didn't even want to go to the dance. All Ava wanted to do now was to go home. She wanted to be alone in her room with her catfish, Tom. She shrunk down into her jacket.

The Mermaid Club had lots of discussions that day. They made plans for the square dance. Ava did not listen very much. When the meeting ended, Ava hurried away without talking to anyone. She swam home by herself.

Chapter Three

Ava was always tall for her age, even when she was a wee mer-baby. Both of her parents were tall. Sometimes, when two parents are tall or short or round, their kids are also tall, short, or round. And so Ava was tall, like her parents. But being tall never bothered Ava until she got teased about it.

There are different types of teasing. Some teasing is gentle. Some teasing is playful.

For example, one day Ava's friend Jenna Scallops said, "Hello there, sea-flower!"

Ava asked, "Why are you calling me sea-flower?"

Jenna answered, "Because you're so tall and beautiful!"

Ava's feelings were not hurt by this, because it was very gentle teasing.

But on another day, someone teased Ava in a way that hurt her feelings.

Ava's class was out on the playground for recess, and they were playing fin-ball, which was a favorite game of merfolk. It was kind of like soccer but also similar to volleyball. The rules aren't important, but a big net was stretched between the two teams. They hit a ball with their tails back and forth into the shell of a big clam, which was called "the goal."

Fin-ball was also a little like basketball, because tall and long merfolk were good players. Short merfolk could be good players, too. Chloe was rather short, but she was still good at fin-ball. However, tall merfolk had long arms and tails. They could easily stretch out and reach the ball and hit it back over the net. Tall merfolk were good at making goals and scoring points.

On this day, Ava's team was winning the fin-ball game. One reason they were winning is that because Ava was so tall, she made lots of points. Almost every time the fin-ball came over the net, Ava smacked it back with her tail.

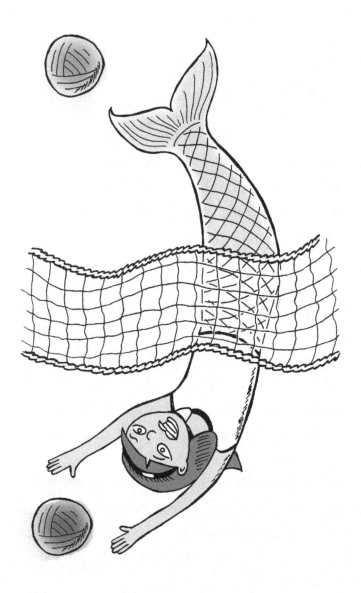

Jack Mackerel, a boy who was on Ava's team, cried, "Nice shot, Ava!"

"Whoo hoo!" yelled Brooklyn Yellowtail, a mermaid who was also on Ava's team.

It was just a fun recess game. Most of the merkids were having lots of fun. However, there was a boy on the other team who was angry. He was angry that his team was not winning. He was angry that Ava was scoring so many points.

He said, "Your team is winning because Ava is tall! That's the only reason! She's so tall, she can't keep her head under water!"

"Yeah," said another merkid. "Passing ships keep ramming into her head because she is so tall!"

Some of the merkids laughed at Ava.

Ava's feelings were hurt. This was not gentle or friendly teasing. It was not nice. Those merkids were making fun of her.

Ava knew they were only jealous of her. She was scoring fin-ball points. However, when it was her turn to serve the ball again, she fumbled the ball and was out of the game.

Ava wished she had been able to think of something clever to say back. Something like, "I'd explain it to you but it would be over your head." Or something like that. But she couldn't think of anything.

And so Ava began to think she might be too tall. She thought she was clumsy. She didn't like the way she looked in her bedroom mirror. Ava had been self-conscious about her height ever since.

Ava knew that they'd only said those things because they were jealous she was winning the game. However, Ava also thought maybe other mers were also thinking about how tall she was.

After that day, it got worse, too. The other mer-kids knew the teasing bothered Ava, so they teased her even more.

She'd get called, "Ava the eel" because she was long and tall. The taunts made her so upset that sometimes she felt like teasing back. She felt like calling them "shorty" or some other mean words to make them stop.

But Ava knew that wasn't the way to solve the problem. Ava had done the right thing to do when you are being teased, which is to ignore it and to swim away.

Why must I be so tall? Ava thought. *It seems like I grow taller every day!*

She'd grown so much in the last couple months. What if she kept growing? Would she be taller than her house? Or taller than the school?

Ava loaded up the family's computer and logged into the Sea-ternet. She started searching online for ways to stop growing.

Just then, Ava's dad swam through the room. He said, "What's up, seashell?"

"Nothing," Ava said glumly. Her Sea-ternet search so far had told her there was no way to stop growing taller.

"Are you watching funny catfish videos?" her dad asked. His name was Marcus, and he was quite tall, too.

"No," said Ava. She turned the computer off.

"Is something the matter?" her dad asked. "You don't seem like your usual happy self."

"It's okay," said Ava. "You can't do anything about it."

"Tell me what's the matter," said Marcus. "Maybe I can help."

"I'm too tall," said Ava, "and I just keep on growing every day."

"Oh, I see," said her dad. He swam close to her. "You know, all mer-kids grow at different rates. I know you've had a growth-spurt recently, but the other mer-kids will grow taller, too."

"But I'll still be one of the tallest," said Ava.

"Of course you will," said Marcus. "That's because I'm tall and your mom is tall. You got your tallness from us. And so in a way, you carry a part of us with you."

"But being tall makes me stand out," said Ava.

"Isn't that a good thing?" Marcus asked.

"Not really," said Ava. "I want to stand out because I'm smart or kind, not because I'm tall."

"I can see that you're really upset about this," said Marcus. "Being different in this way is embarrassing to you."

"Yeah," Ava sighed. "The other mer-kids tease me for being so tall."

"I hate to break it to you, but they would tease you no matter what," said her dad. "They always find something."

Ava thought about this. It was true! There were kids who teased Chloe for being short. And other kids teased Emma for being so quiet.

"You know, Ava" said Marcus, "you do stand out for those good reasons. You are smart and kind. And you're fun to be with, too, especially at parties and picnics. I know that your friends and family think of you as 'Ava the fun mermaid.' Or they think of you as 'Ava the kind mermaid.' We all know there is more about you than only being tall."

"You really think so?" said Ava.

"Come with me for a minute," said her dad. He led Ava outside and then they swam to the surface of the water. "Look up," he said. "What do you see?"

Ava shrugged. The sun was shining brightly and there were fluffy white clouds moving slowly across the blue sky. "The sky. Some clouds."

"Do you see any clouds that are too tall?"

Ava smiled and shook her head.

"How about any ugly clouds? Do you see any ugly clouds?"

"No," said Ava.

"That's right," said her dad. "That's because there's no such thing as a cloud that is too tall or too fat or too anything. There's no such thing as an ugly cloud because clouds are always exactly how they are supposed to be."

It was a beautiful day. Ava blinked up at the sun shining through the clouds.

"And it's the same with you," said Marcus. "You're just exactly how you're supposed to be."

"Okay," said Ava with a chuckle.

"Now, come on. Let's go make some supper," said her dad.

Talking with her dad made Ava feel a little bit better. It was silly to think of a cloud being too tall or not looking good.

And even the Sea-ternet told her that there was

nothing she could do to stop growing tall. But she was still very worried about the dance.

Chapter Four

AT RECESS THE NEXT DAY, Ava looked around at her classmates. She didn't play fin-ball or electric eel tag or any other games. She was hoping that one of her classmates had a growth spurt during the night and had grown taller than she was, or at least as tall as she was. But the other mer-kids all looked the same size.

Chloe swam up to her. "I've been reminding everyone in Mermaid Club about our activity tonight. It's almost time for the big square dance! It's going to be so much fun!"

"Yeah," said Ava dryly. "So much fun."

"Emma is coming to my house before the dance to get ready," said Chloe. "Do you want to come, too?

We're going to put some braids in our hair and pick out some cute tops and colored lip balm."

Ava wanted to be excited and happy, but she wasn't. She would be the tallest mermaid at the dance. There was no doubt about it. She would not be able to find a partner who was shorter than she was. Ava still wanted to go to the dance, but she planned to stay away from the dancing.

"Sure, I'll come to your house," said Ava. "I'll even help you and Emma with your braids."

"I was hoping you'd say that," said Chloe. "I love it when you braid my hair. You're the best braider ever!"

That's because I'm taller than the rest of you, thought Ava.

Chapter Five

AVA HAD PICKED one of her favorite fancy swim tops for the dance. It was sparkly blue and gold. She loved how it looked on her. In fact, Ava almost forgot about how tall she was. Then she swam to Chloe's house. She even felt excited about the square dance. She knew all of her friends would be there, and it would be fun for everyone.

When Ava knocked on the door, Chloe's mother answered. As we said before, sometimes when two parents are tall or short, their kids are tall or short like they are. Chloe was a short mermaid, and so was her mother and father.

Chloe's mother opened the door and then looked

up at Ava. Her eyes got big. Her mouth opened in surprise.

"My, my!" cried Chloe's mom.

"What's the matter?" asked Ava.

"Ava," said Chloe's mom. "You've gotten so tall! My goodness!"

Ava sighed. "Yes, ma'am. I'm having a growth-spurt."

Chloe's mother let Ava into the house. Ava went to Chloe's bedroom. Chloe wore a beautiful magenta top. Emma wore a shimmering white one.

"Braid our hair, Ava!" they shouted. "Please! Braid our hair!"

Ava braided the top part of Chloe's hair in a pattern that looked like flowing water. She also used some special coral beads that were beautiful shades of pale blue and pink. When Ava finished braiding Chloe's hair, she noticed how beautiful Chloe looked.

"What do you think?" Ava asked.

Chloe swam in front of her mirror. "Oh," she said. She sounded a little sad.

"Don't you like the braids?" Ava asked. "I used my special flowing water braid and coral beads. I think you look beautiful!"

"Yes," said Chloe, still looking at herself in the

mirror. "My hair looks fabulous. You really are the best at braiding, Ava," said Chloe.

"Then, what's wrong?" asked Ava.

"Well," said Chloe, "It's just—sometimes I wish I wasn't so short!"

Ava was shocked! She was wishing she wasn't so tall, but Chloe wished she were taller! Ava didn't understand. Ava thought Chloe looked wonderful.

Emma swam over. "I know how you feel, Chloe. I wish I wasn't so shy. There will be so many people there. And lots of loud voices and music. I'm very nervous."

Ava couldn't believe what she was hearing. Emma and Chloe were nervous about the dance, too?

"I've been nervous, too!" said Ava. "I thought I'd stand out because of how tall I am."

"Of course you'll stand out," said Chloe, "because your height is one of the things that make you unique."

"So, all of us were worried about the dance for different reasons," said Ava. She chuckled. "We focus on just one part of us and forget that there's so much more to a mermaid. Like you Chloe, you're so outgoing and vivacious, and Emma you're so kind and easygoing. Wouldn't it be such a different experience if we spent more time thinking about the things we like about ourselves?"

Chloe looked in the mirror again. "True," she said. "I adore these braids. My hair looks mermalicious!"

"And I've always enjoyed square dancing," said Emma. "I think it's so much fun, especially because I don't have to think of the dance moves myself. I just listen to the caller!"

Ava looked in the mirror herself and straightened her posture. "And tall or not," Ava said. "I like myself."

And so the three mermaids swam to the Mermaid Club square dance. It was a short swim, just down the hill at the Fishy Fun Dance Hall.

Some members of the Mermaid Club had volunteered to do the decorations. There were mermagical orbs glowing in purple, blue, and red. A big disco ball made of shiny shells and sea glass reflected beams of colored light onto the walls. Sparkling jellyfish drifted in a circle around the ceiling. Their long shimmering arms hung down like streamers. In one corner of the hall, there was a large table with fancy drinks and snacks. The music was cheerful and fun. Ava, Emma, and Chloe arrived and looked around the dance hall.

"Whoa!" cried Chloe. "The decorations are perfect!"

"Look at all the colors!" yelled Emma.

"Listen to the music!" shouted Ava.

"Wait," said Chloe. "Something's wrong!"

Ava looked around the hall again. Everything seemed perfect. There was just the right amount of jellyfish. The music sounded great. The snacks and drinks looked very yummy!

"What's wrong?" Ava asked Chloe.

"Look!" cried Chloe. "No one is dancing!"

Chapter Six

EVERY MEMBER of the Mermaid Club was at the square dance. And there were lots of merkids at the dance who weren't club members yet. They wanted to come to an activity before they joined. There were also lots of parents at the dance.

And they all looked great!

Brooklyn Yellowtail wore her long blond hair in a high hair-do. She even had little silver minnows to swim in and out of it. Jenna Scallops wore a long cape of silky fabric that waved in the water. Jack Mackerel was wearing a bright green jacket with sparkles on the sleeves. Even the parents had dressed up for the dance.

But Chloe was right. No one was dancing!

Everyone was sitting in the chairs, or hanging out by the snack table. The dance floor was completely empty!

Chloe slapped her forehead and moaned. "Oh, no!" she said. "This is a disaster!"

Ava looked at all the merfolk in the dance hall. They all seemed to be happy. They all seemed to be having fun.

But there was something else. What was it?

Ava saw a group of merkids floating around the snack table. They smiled and sipped their fancy drinks, but they looked nervous, too. Ava saw some other merkids against the wall. They were chatting and smiling, but they looked nervous, also! And there were some merkids who were all alone, not talking to anyone else.

"What in the shark is going on here?" Chloe fretted. "The decorations are perfect! The snacks are perfect! The music is perfect! Why isn't anyone dancing?"

"I know what's going on!" cried Ava. "I know why no one is dancing!"

"Why? Why?" said Chloe and Emma.

"Don't you see?" said Ava. "They're all a little nervous about being at the dance!"

"Huh?" said Chloe.

Ava said, "They're like us! Maybe they're nervous because this is their first dance. Maybe they are nervous because they're by themselves. Maybe they are nervous because they think they are too short, too curvy, or too skinny!"

"Of course!" said Chloe. "They're just like us! Even though they came to the dance, they're all nervous like we were!"

"Exactly!" said Ava.

"But what can we do?" asked Emma. "We can't have a dance with no dancing."

Ava thought about it. She had to do something. She was vice president of the Mermaid Club, after all. Then she remembered that she loved dances and big groups. She loved parties and loud crowds. There was only one thing to do.

"I've got it!" said Ava.

But before Chloe or Emma could say another word, Ava swam away.

"Jack!" Ava shouted. "Welcome to the square dance! I love your jacket! Grab a partner and come to the dance floor!"

Jack set down his fancy snack and said, "Okay!"

"Angie!" said Ava. "Where did you get that swim top? It matches your eyes so perfectly!"

"Thank you, Ava!" said Angie, blushing a little.

"Find a dance partner!" said Ava.

Angie grinned and said, "Okay, I will!"

Ava darted around the room, welcoming the merkids and telling them to dance. Because she was tall, it was easier for her to get their attention. Ava complimented their outfits. She said funny things. She led everyone onto the dance floor.

"Brooklyn, your hair is fabulous," said Ava. "Come dance and show it off!"

"Yeah!" cried Brooklyn, swimming out to the middle of the dance floor. The little silver minnows in her hair-do almost couldn't keep up with her.

Ava realized that if she tried, she could find something good to say about anyone at the dance. *It's easy to tease people about how they act or look,* thought Ava, *but it's just as easy to say something nice!*

Soon a big crowd of merkids and parents were on the dance floor.

Mr. Seagull said, "Okay, everyone! It's time to square dance!"

Goodness! thought Ava. *Look at all these people having fun! This is going to be so great!* Ava didn't notice this, but she wasn't crouching or slouching.

Chloe swam over to Ava. "Ava!" she said, "You're a genius! You saved the Mermaid Club square dance!"

Emma joined them and the three friends swam onto the dance floor. Everyone was swimming into groups of four. Just then, a merboy named Tony swam up next to Ava.

"May I dance with you?" he said.

Oh, seaweed! thought Ava. *Tony is much shorter than I am!*

For one moment, all of Ava's worries came back to her. She suddenly felt nervous again. She had been so nervous about being a tall mermaid with a short dancing partner. But then she looked at Tony. He wore a big smile. He didn't care if Ava was tall and thin or round and short.

Suddenly, Mr. Seagull started a new song. It was time to start the dance. Ava had no time to worry. Everything was perfect just the way it was.

Mr. Seagull was on the microphone. "Bow to your partner, everyone!"

The dancers bowed.

"And now do-si-doe! That means swim back-to-back!"

Everyone swam the do-si-doe. Those who weren't dancing stayed at the edge of the dance floor and clapped along with the music.

The disco ball shimmered. The jellyfish waved their streamer arms through the water.

"Now flippity-flop and turn to your left!" called Mr. Seagull.

Everyone flippity-flopped, then swam together in a circle to the left.

During the dancing, sometimes a merkid would go left instead of right. Or someone would swim up instead of down. Jack went the wrong way and bumped into Brooklyn.

"I'm sorry, Brooklyn!" he said.

"It's okay!" said Brooklyn, laughing.

Jack laughed and shook his head, then joined the dance again.

"You're doing swell, folks!" said Mr. Seagull. His voice boomed through the speakers. He tapped his tail to the music. "Now swing your partner to the right! Swim two backflips and go back to the center!"

The longer the merfolk danced, the better they did. Jack's green jacket sparkled under the mermagical lights. Jenna's flowing cape swept across the dance floor in gentle waves. Even Brooklyn's little silver minnows were dancing!

"Mermaids swim in, and mermen sashay round!" called Mr. Seagull.

As Chloe swung around the dancing square, she spotted Ava and waved at her. Ava waved back. Emma wasn't quite ready to try square dancing yet. Besides, she had to write down everything about the dance. That was her job as secretary. She was over by the snack table with her notebook, but she wore a big smile and gave Ava a big thumbs-up. Also, Tony was a great dancing partner.

The song ended.

"Great job, everyone!" shouted Mr. Seagull. "You dance wonderfully!"

Ava whooped and cheered. Everyone clapped. Mr. Seagull started up a new song, and more merkids and parents came out to the dance floor. Even Emma came out to dance.

"I'll try it once," Emma said with a shy grin on her face.

Ava rushed to the snack table for a fancy drink. She drank it quickly, then popped a fancy snack into her mouth. She was tired from dancing, but she'd forgotten about being tall or getting teased. She only thought about dancing and having fun with her friends from Mermaid Club. Everything was perfectly perfect.

Please leave a review

Thank you for reading this book. I hope you enjoyed it! I would really appreciate it if you would please take a moment to review Ava and the Mermaid Club at the retail site where it was purchased. This helps me to reach new readers. Thank you!

—A.M. Luzzader

WWW.AMLUZZADER.COM

- blog
- freebies
- newsletter
- contact info

About the Author

A.M. Luzzader is an award-winning children's book author who writes chapter books and middle grade books. She specializes in writing books for preteens including *A Mermaid in Middle Grade and Arthur Blackwood's Scary Stories for Kids who Like Scary Stories*

A.M. decided she wanted to write fun stories for

kids when she was still a kid herself. By the time she was in fourth grade, she was already writing short stories. In fifth grade, she bought a typewriter at a garage sale to put her words into print, and in sixth grade she added illustrations.

Now that she has decided what she wants to be when she grows up, A.M. writes books for kids full time. She was selected as the Writer of the Year in 2019-2020 by the League of Utah Writers.

A.M. is the mother of a 12-year-old and a 15-year-old who often inspire her stories. She lives with her husband and children in northern Utah. She is a devout cat person and avid reader.

A.M. Luzzader's books are appropriate for ages 5-12. Her chapter books are intended for kindergarten to third grade, and her middle grade books are for third grade through sixth grade. Find out more about A.M., sign up to receive her newsletter, and get special offers at her website: www.amluzzader.com.

facebook.com/a.m.luzzader

instagram.com/amluzzader

OTHER BOOKS BY
A.M. Luzzader

Mermaid Club: A mermaid girls chapter book

For ages
6-10

OTHER BOOKS BY
A.M. Luzzader

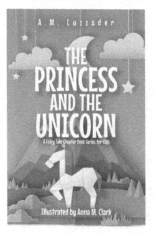 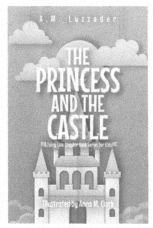

A Fairy Tale Chapter Book Series for Kids

For ages
6-10

OTHER BOOKS BY
A.M. Luzzader

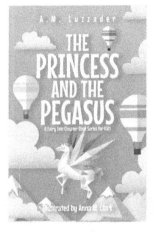 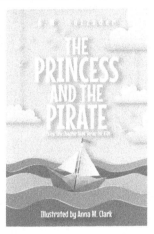

A Fairy Tale Chapter Book
Series for Kids

For ages
6-10

OTHER BOOKS BY
A.M. Luzzader

A Magic School for Girls
Chapter Book

For ages
6-8

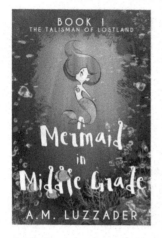

A Mermaid in Middle Grade
Books 1-3

For ages
8-12

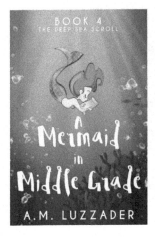 
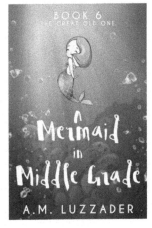

Made in USA - Kendallville, IN
28364_9781949078800
11.07.2023 1420